THE AUTHOR

HEYWARD C. SANDERS

Have previously published his first nonfiction book Equal Rights My Eye, then afterward he published the fiction book Creator, Creation and Betrayal.

I Wish, Why That I Cannot

HEYWARD C. SANDERS

iUniverse, Inc.
New York   Bloomington

iUniverse books may be ordered through booksellers or by contacting:

iUniverse
1663 Liberty Drive
Bloomington, IN 47403
www.iuniverse.com
1-800-Authors (1-800-288-4677)

Because of the dynamic nature of the Internet, any Web addresses or
links contained in this book may have changed since publication and may
no longer be valid. The views expressed in this work are solely those of
the author and do not necessarily reflect the views of the publisher, and
the publisher hereby disclaims any responsibility for them.

ISBN: 978-1-4502-5391-8 (sc)
ISBN: 978-1-4502-5393-2 (ebook)

Printed in the United States of America

iUniverse rev. date: 08/31/2010

TABLE OF CONTENTS

A Note From The Author

This is a fictional story is about a person that lives in a society, where he was not happy with the choices that were put in front of him.

By being program as a kid from his parents to reject the changes that was happening with the society he live in, he lost a lot of communication with his friends.

Life for him became real difficult, for him to function with the people that were always a part of his life that he has been use to being around with.

By growing up made their language of talking, and the lifestyles that they liked change to a way that they did not understand each other anymore, which made them dislike each other more and more.

Because of all the things that their parents did around them, had made a big effect to their relationship with each other.

They had to separate their self from each other before it got to far out of hand. By separating from his friends he realizes through meeting new people, it seems like that everybody he come across, had some ways more like his friends he left behind, easy to be influence to go against what they know is right.

Life for him and some of the ones he was raise up with went a different way from the way they was raise up to be, and life start to changing for them in a way that they was not brought up to be, things became more difficult but they found away to deal with the problems they put their selves in.

Later on in his life he started drifting further and further into isolation, away from everybody accepts his family.

He stopped communicating with a lot of people that he know, and did not want to do anything but find away to make money without being around people that he did not trust anymore.

He start enjoying his life with a different crowd of people that he was not use to knowing, by doing just the little things in life with the new crowd he meet, they made him realize that he took life for granted when he was running with the wrong crowd, and the more he got comfortable with his new *life, the more he became a threat to the government and others who was a part of the establishment.*

This story will show you why he took a drastic change in his life, and did not try to adjust to the changes that society was gone through that the government allowed the business world, do to the people in his country, and by he refuse not to play a part of that lifestyles that was before him, his eyes open up to all the tricks that his government have, to influence the people of his country.

Problems that he seen around his community's, forced him to try and find away to take action in bringing the people back into consciousness, so they will be able to restore their neighborhoods back in order, for the future of their children's and the children's to come.

And what made him isolate his self from everybody, which was a part of his life; he was adjusted to why growing up.

Thanks for taken the time out to read this story, and I hope it will be a mind opening for parents that making decisions with their kids life.

CHAPTER ONE

I Wish That I Could Hang On The Corner

Once upon a time, there was a kid that had grown up in a community, where he was surrounded with a lot of friends that play together.

At seven years old; all he did was hang around with his friends in the neighborhood, and had a lot of fun being with them.

They went to school together; play sports, and hanging around the school play ground together, doing everything and anything that they could do just to have fun.

They even share a lot of things like toys, and candy, and money together when they can, some had the benefits of getting allowances from their parents, and the others had to go out in the community, and take orders at the grocery store to be able to have the benefits the other kids have.

But how every they receive it they still found away to look out for each other.

Their loyalty; for each other was not questioned, they care and worry about what one were doing and who was with them at that time, they acted like siblings more then friends. Their parents gave them a lot of responsibilities, in taking care of the thing that are important to them, and made them follow the rules that they put down for them.

But some was not fortunate to have parents that were gone to control their life in everything they were doing.

Those were the ones that had to take orders at the grocery store, to get money to stay on the level with their friends.

It was hard for their parents to give them and allowance all the time, because their jobs did not afford them to do the things that the other parents could do with their kids.

But those kids understood what their parents were going through, and try to do everything in their power not to ask them for much.

The ones that did not have much, their parent still spend a lot of time with them, talking and playing together.

One of the kids who parents did not have much, always took time out to explain to him the things that life have to offer him, and to appreciate the little things in life, because one day they will be gone.

They also reminded their kid that things is not always what it seem to be like, and the things that make you proud can turn on you and make you sad.

The father said; to his son what ever you do through life, things going to come in your path that you would not understand, and the only way to beat it is to stay true to yourself, at all time and always try to be the bigger person to walk away from trouble when you can.

All the kids had good parental supervision and at the school, parents and teacher meeting, their parents had a chance to meet with each other, and get to know one another, and see what the teachers thought about their kids and the friends that they keep company with while they are in school, see by the parents working all the time they never had a chance to really have a one on one conversation with their neighbors.

At the parents and teacher meeting, the parents started separating their selves, doing the times when they meet up at the parents and teachers meeting.

The parents that thought they made more money "the white collar," had more in common with each other they started communicating more, and the parents that wore *uniforms, that was consider as "blue collar worker" they started communicating more with each other.*

Just that little move made a big change in how their kids thought about each other, and started acting out in a different way with each other.

But the biggest problem started, by them being kids they did not understand what was happening to their relationship with each other.

Just trying to get approval from their parents of whom they think were good for them to play with, just that itself made a different in how the kids act towards each other.

The parents wanted full control of which kids they spend all their time with, and made it known of what friends that they the parents approve of for their kids to play with. When the kids come over to play, the parents put a lot of time in to the kids that their parents has similar lifestyle with, the other kids can feel that the parents are more comfortable in talking to the child, with the parents who have more in common with them.

The kids started changing; and was doing the same things that their parents was doing unconsciously to each other, than they started picking what friend that they would spend time and share their things with.

They even started going to school separate and hanging on the play ground separate, the relationship they once have had took a turn for bad, and they started talking about one another.

They still hung around on the corner with each other, but separate in groups and always trying to crack jocks on each other, using that as a sneaky way to speak of how they feel about that person.

Now when they play sports together it's one group against the other group, they still liked each other in a different way, but the things that their parents did had created a move swing with them that they had no knowledge of what was happening to them.

And when some time if a group that is comfortable with each other, see one of the kids that they do not hang around a lot with anymore, coming down the street they will hide from him or say that they had to go in the house.

And when one of the kids are at home, and one of the kids come and knock on their door that he really do not want to play with, he will tell his parents to say that he is sleep.

The parent says nothing about what he just did because it's not one of the kids that they be communicating with *parents, but the little kid out side that door can feel that they is not wanted there anymore and he stop coming by.*

Time permitted them to grow up hanging on that same corner, with so many differences in how they feel about each other, but forced to ignore them for now, they tolerated each other because they was from the same neighborhood, and strange as that seem they knew that together they was strong, and divided they would be picked on.

That was the only reason that they did not separate earlier, because the other kids in the other areas knew that they all ran together, and if you mess with one you mess with them all.

When they reached junior high school, they started drifting a part from each other, because some went to different schools and met with other kids from a different area, and started hang around with them on their corner.

Before you know it they were seeing each other just in passing, the two groups that separate their self went their separate ways.

Now their parents recognize that the kids they are hanging around with are different kids, and they see that their kid personality had changed in a big way, they acted so different that their parents did not understand the new them.

Their parents could tell everything they were doing in school, and what kind of crowd they were being with, because of their grades.

Some of the kids brought home bad grades, and stay in trouble at school, some of the kids was just making it through school with just fair grades, and you had a few kids just stop going and start hanging out side the school, trying to be cool with the kids they thought was bad.

The parents did not understand why these things were happening, so they started blaming everybody accepts their selves, for their kids problem and the things they was going through.

It became some hard years that the parents went through with their kids in junior high school, kids arguing back with the parents throwing thing around the house, locking their room to keep their parents out and threaten to hurt their self.

Things got hard for the parents they started withdrawing from each other and began arguing more with each other. They were so hurt in what was going on with their child that they started turning on each other, some parents started drinking heavy and the life they once knew was a thing of the past.

One of the kids parent that was a blue collar worker die, he were drinking real heavy one day, and fell the sleep while he was smoking in bed, and the bed caught on fire, he was the only one at home doing that time, and burned the house up. When the fire trucks came it was to late for the father, the smoke destroy him first, by he being in the bed room with the door close, and the fire finished him off and that kid was not the same anymore.

He started getting locked up at a young age, and every time he got out, he will go and do something to put himself right back, stealing out of a store or doing something that make no sense.

"Then one of the kids parent was stubbed to death, he were drinking with a friend hanging on the corner, and they started arguing about something and the man took out his knife and stubbed the kids father about five time, those kids was not the same anymore the older ones started working to pay the bills and to keep food on the table for the family. Things were changing fast they both, the kids and parents, were feeling the effects of life."

"Then another parent die at home, he was also a blue collar worker when he was having dinner with his family, the father chocked on a bones and those kids was not the same anymore, it was a girl and boy child, they started hanging out with a different crowd in another neighborhood."

The kids that had white collar worker as parents they did not see them often, because their parents stay at work, or the mother run the house movement.

One was a doctor that stay at work all the time, he was on call from day and night, and one was a preacher that work for the federal government, and the others worked with the government in office positions.

They had their problems to some was drinking so hard that they started physically abusing their family, fighting with his wife for no reason, and smacking his kids around for no reason.

And there were one that who was cheating on his wife at work, and was messing around in the neighborhood with young girls that were his older kid age.

Then the kids; start hearing things about one of the kid mother was caught having sex, with the slick number backer parent while the father was at work.

And rumors came out on some of the kid's mothers that they were sleeping together with each other.

The truth started pouring out, and every adult was moving around the community real light, to scare to say anything thinking that some one has something on them that will get back to their family and mess up they house whole.

The years made the community get real bidder and secretive, the trust one had with the adults change when a lot of information started pouring out more and more, the kids lost a lot of respect for their parents, and started walking around the community with their head down.

A lot of them stop hang out or talking with the people in the areas, they went out to hang in other areas and came home just to sleep.

To scare to crack a jock with the kids in the area where they live at, when they run across each other on the block, or around the neighborhood, thinking about the things that they know, worried about if they will say something about their parents of what they did that everybody know.

When the kids seen each other they was happen for that moment, because they was thinking about the things that they did when they was young, to scare to say anything about what went wrong, so they talk a while and smile and then they went on their own way.

CHAPTER TWO

I Wish That I Could Party All The Time

The last year in junior high school the kids that was still going, they started fighting all the time and running with gangs beating up other kids, and one of the kids was getting beaten up by their own gang.

The gang knew that he was not like them, and they took the cold blooded average over the kid, because he was just trying to fit in with everybody.

But the kid that stop going the school, and started hang out side the school on the corner, he was the one who were taking order at the grocery store, and when he got older he started serving papers to earn money to take care of his personal needs, trying to keep up with the other kids that their parents was able to do for.

He was the kid that his father uses to set down with and talk to him about life challenges that is gone to come his way one day.

He was a little more street smarter then the other kids he play with, he was good in making money and knew what to do with it.

When he was a little boy taking order at the grocery store, he use to save his money and loan it out to his father friends for a quarter on a dollar, his mind was like a calculator machine that be scheming all the time.

He also was the aggressive one that was well liked in the community, if trouble come his way he were smart enough to take control over it before it got out of hand, and also knew how to keep gangs from fighting with each other.

Everybody talked with him about everything that was going on in school and around the community.

That's when he found out that one of his childhood friends was being taking bad by the gang that he was hanging with. Even thro they did not hang together anymore and had some differences with each other, he still feel obligation to look out for his old friends.

Because when they were going through their changes, his father told him not to blame his friends for the things that happen to you all, because they did not have control of the poison that was pushed in their heads by their parents.

He went to talk to the kid that was getting beaten up, the kid was glad to see him, and they smile at each other, and then he told the kid that he was not raise like the crowd that he were hanging with, and that he can do better then that, because they the crowd, he was hanging with was gone to use him up and might get him locked up like their friend that stay in and out of jail.

The kid; that was getting beaten up all the time was so happy, that his old friend took the time to come and see if he was all right.

Just that talk with his old friend change a lot of things that he was doing, and he started back getting his grades back up in school, and stop hanging around with that crew that did not mean him any good.

The gang; did not like the kid when he stopped talking to them, and wanted to do something to him.

But they had a visitor that told them if they mess with his old friend he will be back to see them.

The gang; knew that he was liked with all the gangs because he was the one that kept the peace; with everybody, they did not want any trouble with him so they left the kid alone.

13

The kid that was being beaten up by the gang never knew that his old friend went to talk with the gang to get him out.

The kid that was getting beaten up felt so good about his old friend still care about him, and he knew if the gang tried to do something to him that his old friend will be there with him.

So they all went on with their life and started partying a lot, messing with the girls, and playing sports for the school. Their last year in junior high school made them wiser, and taught them how to adapt to the situations that will come their way.

When they reached high school they was juniors all over again, but this time they knew how to act and who to be around, the ones that stay in school, ended up playing sports for the high school, and was playing real good as a junior, some of them was starting first string on the team.

The kids; that stop going the school they was growing up in the street world and became real deep in to the hustling game, and started doing all kinds of crimes just to be look at as being cool.

Than they started; messing with the young fast girls in the street, they knew that they needed a lot of money to keep them around.

"Than the young kids started; selling drug to stay cool and almost every young kid in school wanted to be like them, but were to scare because they know that their parents would be mad with them.

As the years went on their parties started getting out of control, kids was being shot in the parties, and also when they were walking home from the parties."

Kids; was taking other kids cloths off their backs taking their shores off their feet's.

But the kids that was in the street if they knew who you were then everything was all right, you did not have to worry about trouble from them.

The kids that stop going the school their whole life became hustling and partying, they moved up from house parties, to going to clubs and discos, that crowd was more harder then the house party crowd, you might run in to one of your enemies at any time.

Kids in the night clubs was partying all night and the girls was hooking up with some of the gangs, and they had ended up at a motel or hotel with some gangs that they did not even know.

The kid that stop going the school and started hustling; was hanging around the school with the other young kids, just to find some girls that wanted to hook school, and go with them to party at one of the kids houses while their parents was at work, the fast girls wanted to be cool and like hanging out around with the bad boys, that give the girls a little of a repetition in school as being cool girls.

Life started getting hard for the young street kids, the older hustler seen the opportunity to use the young hustlers in making more money, they recruited them in robbing store and burglaries houses, the older hustlers already had the young hustlers selling drug for them.

"And the older hustlers; use to get the young hustlers to get the young girls at school to hook school so they can have sex with them to, it look like that the young hustlers was making a lot of money, but the other kids did not know that all the money was going to the older hustlers who was controlling them."

"The older hustlers; let the young hustlers use their cars to ride around the school, to recruit more young kids to hustle for them, and pick up young girls to have sex with them, and they will be getting out of some of the bad it's cars that will attract a lot of attention to them, every kid that wanted to be cool, or every girl that wanted to be with a bad boy, were flocking around them trying to do anything they wanted them to do."

The kids; that stop going the school and start hanging around school, they did not see their old friends, that came from their community with them for a long time, they started going to different parties, the school kids was still going to house parties, and the kids that stop going the school they was going to clubs and discos.

It was about six month to a years before they ran into each another, and when they did see each other they always smile because they was glad to see one another, and stop to talk about the things they use to do when they was young, and asked how some of the others was doing, then they embraced each other and then went their own way.

CHAPTER THREE

I Wish That I Could Drink And Drug Everyday

The older hustlers; wanted more power over the young hustlers; they got the young hustlers to start drinking.

Then the older hustlers started knocking some of the young hustlers around when they did something wrong.

Before you knew it the older hustlers had the young hustlers messing with marijuana, they was smocking it all the time and things got out of control, they was making a lot of mistakes when they went out to commit a crime that the older hustlers planed for them.

"One day the young hustlers made a mistake and came back without any money, the older hustlers were mad and shot one of the young hustlers that made them mess the capper up, and return back with no money."

The older hustlers; did not care about the safety of the younger hustlers all they care about was the money.

The kid; that stop going the school that came from the community with the other kids, he would go out with them once an a while, because he was doing good selling drugs for the old hustlers, and the older hustlers respected him a lot because he could think and knew how to make money. But when the young hustler was shot by the older hustlers that kid did not know about what really happen to him.

"He thought that it happen coming out of one of the robberies they did.

To one day they were so high from drinking and smocking marijuana, and one of the young hustlers started arguing about what the young hustler did that got him shot."

It was the first time for the kid that was well liked from all the gangs to hear what really went down, "he got mad and asks them what really happen?"

They told him that the young hustler made a mistake and the owner got the jump on him, and they had to drag him out and get away from the seam of the crime.

"The kid that everybody liked; he was still aggressive but just was caught up doing what the rest of the young hustlers were doing, getting high off of drugs and drinking."

"He approach; the older hustlers of what he heard that happen to the young hustler, and the older hustlers told him to mind his business and for him to not to get in their business again."

The young hustler knew what that meant and started scheming with the young hustlers, and start breaking away from the older hustlers control over them.

See the kid that everybody liked he was working with the older hustlers just to learn the game any way, then he was going to take the young hustlers with him and start their own organization, the time just came earlier then he wanted it to be, because he really did not like what just happen to the young hustler and being threaten by them.

He felt; that he was in the same position his old friend from the neighborhood that was in, when he had to confront the gang at school about him.

So he started scheming; with the young hustlers and was getting all the guns that they could get from the older hustlers, and started buying some off the street, they ended up with so many guns that they was ready to do anything that needed to be done.

One day the older hustlers; purchase a lot of drugs and the young hustlers knew when it suppose to come, and where they was going to stash it.

The young hustlers had masked their face in case something went wrong, and the older hustlers could not prove that they were the ones that robbed them.

"When the older hustlers; walked up to where they were stashing their drugs at, the younger hustlers jumped out on them and took their drugs, then one of the older hustlers reached for his gun, and the young hustler that they shot for making a mistake when they send the young hustlers on a capper, shot the older hustler about four times, and they took all the drugs and money from the older hustlers and left."

The older hustlers; knew that it was the younger hustlers who rob them that work with them, but was to scare to say anything because they seen how powerful they have became, so the older hustlers tried to get on their good side and started sharing a lot of their power with them.

"The young hustlers; seen how weak the older hustlers was and started rebelling on them, and told the older hustlers that they had to give them all the drugs, they was selling in

there area, and they would pay them only thirty percent of the profits?"

"The older hustlers did not like it but went along with them for now, unto they was able to make plan on how to get them out of their way."

One thing the younger hustlers; did not know was the older hustlers had to answer to some body that kept them safe, and that was the "police officers" that ran the communities.

"Police officers; approached the young hustlers, and told them what they had to do for them."

The young hustlers; got mad at the older hustlers for snitching on them.

Because the older hustlers; was the ones that told them about never to be a snitcher, but they turned around and put the "police officers" on them.

"The young hustlers; started scheming on the older hustlers, and ended up shooting all of the older hustlers and went wild in the street."

They did not care about the "police officer," and was not gone to make a deal with them.

"They started; robbing all the older hustlers in every area because they knew that they was working with the police officers," they in up hating all the older hustlers every wear *and started recruiting more young hustlers to take over all the areas in their city.*

"They started; robbing banks and armor trucks they got so powerful that the new media and the chief of police were talking about them all the time, in how to stop the crime in the area that got out of control."

"The police officers started cracking down on the young hustlers, a lot of them got locked up, and some was killed, and some was on drugs real bad, and started snitching on the others.

It took about a year or more before the street was back in order again, and the police officers recruited some more older hustlers, that just came home from doing a lot of time for drugs, that they had control over before, and the older hustlers recruited some of the hustlers that was locked up with them, to put in the position to make money for them.

Mostly all the strong young hustlers was locked up and the weaker young hustlers was left with the new older hustlers, to be manipulated to do their work for them.

The weaker hustlers was real happy to get the opportunity to be powerful in the communities, they finally had a chance to get the girls that they always wanted, even if the girls was burn out and on drugs, the weaker hustlers and the hustlers that came home from jail could not see that, all they could see in their eye's was the girls when they was young, who they always had a crush on but could not get them because they was not in the right circle."

The bad part about the burn out girls, and the weaker hustlers, and stupid hustlers, they did not like for people to call them who they really was, if some one call the burn out girls a freak, and the weaker hustlers suckers or the stupid hustlers stupid, they will try to get some body to try and hurt the person or persons for saying that.

It got so bad that the good man's and woman's was so confuse, the city made them think that they was wrong in the way they were action, and the backward life was the right way to be.

And the city got worse the weaker younger hustlers, and the stupid hustlers just came home from jail was running the city, for the older hustlers that was running the city, for the police officers, and everybody started snitching on each other, and the hustling game got so bad that good hustlers, was getting out of the business and started working real jobs to take care of their families.

There was no real money in the street because the weak hustlers and the stupid hustlers that came home from jail would take anything just to get by, so the street became a drug user's world the prices was "cheaper and the drugs was stronger" and it affected the whole city.

"All the weak hustlers and stupid hustlers recruited their weak friends that always wanted to be in the game, they was coming from jail, the ones that was locked up for petty and stupid crimes, and from private schools, from colleges, from government jobs, walking on streets that was forbidden for them to be on in the older days."

"It started effecting the city and everybody in the city started having petty minds in everything they did, they started hustling on the street where they was raise at, and a lot of them was hustling right on their family pouch, the city had a epidemic of no respect for nothing but faking that became a style, they was still working in government jobs and going the school but they started thinking how to do things in a petty way, and the city went down."

"They was not strong enough to keep the out side forces from taking over the city, people was coming from other cities and started setting up shop there, before you knew it people was coming from other countries coming in and taking over everything."

One of the drug user that use to run with the young hustlers, that was locked up he remember an old saying he always heard (never give a sucker an even break and never hip a lame to the game), and then he said to others now I know why they say that.

Before you knew it the cities all over the country was controlled by people that came from other countries, they started getting all the drugs from their countries and the weaker hustlers and stupid hustlers opened the door up so wide that they thought the country was theirs to do anything they wanted to.

"Then the peoples in the cities got lazy and stop doing the work on their jobs and the private companies and the government started replacing them with others from different countries.

It gotten out of control the weaker and stupid ones messed up everything the cities had to offer a person when they grow up and look for a job.

Jobs were leaving the country and the country depended on other countries to feed them and cloth them, the country stop making things to take care of their selves they was ninety percent depended on other countries for everything."

"The recession hit and everybody did not know what to do, the big companies made it possible for the "weaker and stupid peoples" in the cities to get a jobs, because they knew they did not care about nothing but funning and having their toys to play with.

They knew that they were the easiest ones to win them over to get in the country and take control over it.

And the "police officers" did not care about who run the country, as long as they think that the country is being control by them, and their money kept coming in for them."

Peoples that was coming from other countries started paying the "police officer" to watch things for them and the "police officers never mist a beat," it got more better for the "police officers," because they was dealing direct with the peoples that was controlling everything.

"The police officers and the weaker and stupid hustlers had a lot in common they both did not care about the state of the country; all they wanted was to look important so the females can like them.

The police officers and the weak and stupid hustlers and the burn out males and females were happy with their position, because the big companies from other countries gave them good positions at work and on the street, the country went down real bad and a recession became a depression and nothing was safe anymore."

CHAPTER FOUR

I Wish That I Could Give My Responsibilities To Somebody Else

---

A lot of people lost their job and things went wild everybody was robbing, just to pay a bill and to feed their families, good strong worker that was on their job for years who had principles, they was laid off, because they were not gone to stand for what the new companies was doing to the country.

"It was like an epidemic peoples were getting laid off their jobs because the companies were going out of business, and new companies were coming in with new worker from other countries, that they train to run the weaker worker that was still working with the companies."

People that worked all their life on one job was so stress out of what just happen to them, and did not know how to deal with it.

"Some went home and kill their whole family."

"Some started shooting anybody."

"And some just killed their self," the country went crazy for a while and the government official step in and promise them that the country is getting better, and people started calming down.

The government sold false hope to the peoples and they laid down waiting for something to happen, it was hard for the government to tell the country that they fail them and took their eye off the job that the people elect them to do. The government started playing all sorts of games trying to keep the country calm to they find away to get things back in order, but in reality their government official's minds knew that nothing good were not gone to happen for his country.

"See the government knew how to play with society every five years, when the kids graduate from college, the government put in position the college kids to get good jobs, and get the old worker to take a buy out with a good monthly check.

The college kids did not know anything about a recession because they were in school, and nine out of ten of their parents or the government loans were paying their way through.

Their responsibilities came when they finest school and had to pay that loan back, some did not have a loan because their parents took care of that with trust fun money for hard times.

And some got their school loan deferred for two to five years be for they had to start paying on it."

Then the government; started bailing companies out with other countries money, and they became deeper and deeper depending on other countries to help them.

The country money value went down and the government was making money as fast as they can print it for their country, and they became the number one counterfeiters in the country.

See the people did not care as long as the counterfeit money was coming in every month, the people did not mist a beat they was so condition to function one way that they could not see what was happening to them.

They believed in their government official they elected to run the country, and was praying that things get better for them.

The government; made everybody depended on counterfeit money, they put able body people on food stamps that really wanted to work, but the government was covering up the wrong that they did, by letting people from other countries get the job that able body people in that country wanted.

But the big companies that were controlling the country did not want the stronger people that were born there to work for them.

The government; did not want to tell the people that they put the country in the worse conditions and it's nothing that can be done about it.

"See the government know if the countries that his country owe call their debt in, the country could not pay them, the foreign countries they owe was not gone to take the counterfeit money that the government was printing every day, and they country did not have enough of gold or expensive minerals to pay the debt.

The only way they could pay the debt is give the country up to all lenders or go the war, and their government was not trying to go the war against the lenders.

See their country use to pay the debts they owe by protecting the countries they owe, but the biggest debt that they owe do not need their protection, their army was just as bigger then theirs and stronger, they put their people and country in a check mate."

Then a lot of males that lost their jobs started moving in with female that still had good income, and the female started talking to the males like they was little kids and ordering them around calling them all kinds of names, the males got use to it and adjusted because they did not have no wear to go.

It was sickened for a man to see that, and they refuse to be in those conditions like the way they seen the other males that was being treated by a female, that they might have helped them when she was down.

Those female watching their bosses at work and dreaming about a man like them, of how they take care of their lady.

But never consider that if their boss loses their job they will be doing the same things the males doing that living with them, but their woman might recognize the good things he did, when he was able to do, when he was working.

A lot of man's became creative and made their way in taking care of their self, they was smart enough to let go everything and kept the bear necessities and started all over again.

It was hard at first for them because they was condition to the good thing that they worked hard for, but they understood that desperate time brings desperate situations and they started adjusting to their new conditions.

And the young kids that was coming from college going into the working world some of the female were doing all right with trust fund money, and their male friends started staying with them and got use to being depended on their female, they was like their mothers and the young males did not care, they thought that it was not to bad because they was in love, but the females was sick of them and their ways.

CHAPTER FIVE

I Wish That I Can Be A Lover To All The Girls

The country went out of control disease was spreading all over the country, the weak hustlers and the stupid hustlers that was messing with the burn out females, who was walking around with all kinds of disease, and start pasting them on to the weak and stupid hustlers.

"The weak and stupid hustlers; spread it to all the young girls in school who wanted to be fast," "and the young fast girls spread it through the school with the sport players," "and the sport players spread it to their girl friends that they was with."

"It became an epidemic; all through the land the old and the young was not safe."

"The government; had everybody on sex so bad that they were out of control."

The government; had to find a way to give the country up with out the people noticing what really was happening to the country.

"The people; in that country high gene went down and germs started spreading more," "some people that was sharing nettles that know they had a disease did not care if they give it to somebody else."

"And some girls; that look real good made it their business to go in clubs just to spread it on purpose, because somebody gave it to them on purpose," so they was mad and did not care who they give it to.

"And the males; especially the weak and stupid hustlers they spread it around like it was a candy that everybody like," they had no respect for life everything was a jock to them.

"Then the gay communities; start spreading it so fast because a lot of males was messing with both sex male and female," bring diseases home to their wife or a live in girl friend, it got so out of control that it became normal and people did not care about catching it anymore.

The government; had everybody on some kind of treatment for the disease, and they start taking all kinds of medicine.

The government put the communities in a robotic way; the people never questioned anything the government was doing to them.

The government; know what they was doing to the people in that country, because when a group start speaking about what the government was doing, the government charge them for trying to over throw the country and they then got silent, and start talking about the government in a way that was not a threat to what the government are doing to their country.

The cities had a dark cloud over them every one was on some kind of medication the old and the young,

"Kids was young as five years old was taking medication and the government were paying their parent a month for a disable kid," people did not care about the ware fare of their child, all they wanted was that check every month for a slow child, the parents became the rotten it's parent in the history of that country, using their child as a experiment for the government to slow the process of progress of their communities down.

"The normal kids that was getting the check every month started acting like something was wrong with them," because they was on the medication so long they got program to think like that.

"Then when they got older to go out in the community to find a job," they did not know how to function at their work place, "that itself made them really think that something was wrong with their self," just because their parents used their kids for a check to hustle the government because they did not want to work.

Chapter Six

I Wish That I Could Be Gay

Before you know it the country was taking another political turn, a movement was rising and the country had to hear them out, they got so strong that the government had to bow down to them. They had all the high position jobs in the government and a lot of old money that was left to them, they took over the entertainment world, and the news media, the radio stations, the private companies, and the government.

The country had to step back and let them in because if they take their money out of the country, their country would have fallen over night.

The gay movement; change that country so fast that people refuse to adjust to those ways, people started losing jobs because they did not like how their gay boss was talking to them, if your body looked like or was thinking about to say something against the movement, the government gave them so much power to bring you down by any means necessarily.

A lot of people was scare to talk out because they know that they will lose their job, then the country went silent people was smiling just to try to get a long with the gays.

They had so much power; they will let you know it, and when they walk through the communities they will say anything or do anything and people just smile.

"If they tell the community not to like a person then that person will not be liked," "and when they do anything around the neighborhood that do not look good people act like they did not see it."

"The country became a gay heaven for them and everybody else was their servants to wait on them hand and foot."

The government push this lifestyle down the people throats to fast and the country became divided in so many ways, people did not trust the government anymore and people was so scare to talk when they went on a interview for a job, and supervisors was scare to interview gays because if they did not higher them they can file for discrimination when they was not qualify for the job.

It came on the country to fast and people was not adjusted for the quick change, a lot of families ended up falling out with each other because they never know that a member was gay, it were so many people that was in the closet came out and shocked their families. "People who had big families with a lot of kids came out the closet," "and some who had stand in friends to make their family think that they was normal," a lot of family stop talking and the trust level when down with everybody, people was scare to talk about subject because they did not know "anymore who they was talking to and did not want to offend each other beliefs."

CHAPTER SEVEN

Wish That I Could Follow The Crowd

Ten years have pasted since the young hustlers was locked up, and they were still doing time in the institutions, other gangs recruited them, some joined with religions, and some joined militant groups, some was running with crews that were robbing and raping other prisoners for drugs and sex, some just went to school and was going back and forward to the law library to learn law.

They all stay in shape lifting weights and running around the track field and some played sports to past the time, because they had about five more years to go before their time was up. But the leader that was smart and ran the gangs he stay to his self and got deep into his thoughts, he wanted to get back to the ways that he was taught by his parents, and take the advantage of all the things he could learn that can help him when they return back into society.

All the gangs in the institutions still have a lot of respect for him because he was always able to think for his self, and he decide not to follow any crowd why he was incarcerated, because he was still messed up of what the older hustlers did to them and made the situation happen like it did.

He did not trust the crew that got locked up with him anymore because they was following groups for the wrong reason, he knew that they were not gone to be with that lifestyle when they return to the street. He thought that they were scare of being their self thinking that somebody might try to do something to them.

He had his trouble with other inmates while being there but came out more respected and stronger with the inmates incarcerated with him. All he did is exercise and went to the law library to learn law and business on his own, and done the work that was assign to him, and stay in his block so he would not have to much communication with the officers that is controlling the institution.

He still did not like the police officers because he thought that they was the problem to societies sickness, he knew that it was some police officers that was bringing things in to prison, and were putting inmate on other inmate if they did not do what the officers wanted them to do. He knew that the things that were going on in the prisons were created by the officers and that they are running things like the officers was running thing in the street.

His parents always came to see him, and told him some things that was happen in the neighborhood where he was raise at, and the things they was doing with their life, his mother was still working on the same job and his father retire and open a business, he open a heath food store with his credit and his wife credit, and they got a little loan that they could pay back, and with the money they save up that their son gave them for their selves, they saved up a pretty amount to do anything that they wanted to do.

He was so happy that his parents were still positive because it was hard to talk to positive people where he was at, because he knew they were faking about the things that they was talking about and when they return back to society ninety nine percent of them will be doing the same things that they say they were against on the street.

CHAPTER EIGHT

Why That I Can Not Hang On The Corner

Five years have pasted and the young hustlers was coming out one by one, and they started moving around seeing how things were, they realize that things changed real bad, all the young kids that was scare and school kids were running the streets and telling stories like they use to run with them, telling stories to the new young hustlers about the things they did to control the city. And the new young hustlers thought that the weak hustler that was telling the story was the bosses over the ones that were coming out.

The new young hustlers was looking at the ones that was coming home from prison that use to work for their bosses, thought they would have to give their position up back to them which they refuse to do.

It was so crazy and the young hustlers were dumber and dangerous because they could not think, and it was easy for them to be manipulated by the weak and stupid hustlers to do anything for them. Some of the ones came out from prison got kill by the new young hustlers because they started trying to make the weak hustlers pay them money, some became flunkeys for the weak and stupid hustlers that are in control of their city now.

But the one who parents started their own business with some of the money he gave to them, he knew that was gone to happen when they come out, because when they was incarcerated they did not prepare their self for when they return back into society.

And he ran into some older friend from the neighborhood where he was raise, and they told him that the kid that he had to talk to the gang for him to get out of became a boss to the new young hustlers; he could not believe the things that is happening around the city and who was in charge now.

"All his life he had been fighting against the weak and stupid hustlers who were working for the weak older hustlers that were working for the police officers.

And now he back home and everything is back in the same order that his crew fought against, a lot of his crew went to jail with him was trying to get him to come out and start the gang back."

But he knew that they were not the same because he did time with them and seen that they was easy to be influence by other people who they thought was somebody.

Then his old friend that he protected from the gang came to him and asked to join his crew and he will give him anything he wanted?

"He could not believe what his old friend was saying to him because they knew that you could not buy him."

"They looked into each other eyes, and the old friend seen, that is a boss to the young hustlers knew he made a mistake in asking him that," the old friend apologize to him and told him that will never happen again, and they smile at each other and talk a little and then went on their way, that was the last time he seen him and a lot of his old friends from the neighborhood, unless they came into his father store where he was working at.

His loyalty was only to his family and no one else because he know the things he did was wrong that coursed him to get locked up, getting high on your own product was wrong and running with a crowd that did not mean him any good, it was his first time in along time that he had peace with his self. He knew that his parents would not bring any harm to him and will watch his back a hundred percent.

CHAPTER NINE

Why That I Can Not Party Anymore

A lot of his old friends from the neighborhood would come around the store shopping, and was trying to get him to come out and go to some parties with them. He refuses because he did not have time to do anything but work on how to make his family business more successful. Everybody knew he was a extremists in everything he do, and like things to be organize so that they can be easy to find when the customers was looking for them. He got so into the store time started moving before you knew it a year past, he started rearranging the store and was doing the books to keep the count on everything that was being sold, so they will know what to buy that is getting low. His parents was so glad that he decide to work with the family business, because they was not making enough to hirer some one to work in the store and pay a accountant to do their books, and pay all their debts that was created by opening the store.

"His studying when he was in prison came in handy for the family, he taught them about the things that they could write off on taxes, and told them that the government was doing illegal acts to the people in the country, and the accountants are not saying anything about it.

Then he explain to his parents that people are paying taxes on things that they can write off on tax at the end of the year, because they are being taxed two time for the same money that they take out taxes from their jobs, they need to keep every receipt and at the in of the year write everything off, and he said I mean everything that their money was used for, that was taking out of their checks for taxes at work state and federal. And all the things that they his parents can write off from their store they was not writing off and his mother job she was not writing off.

Then he showed them how to get the best merchandise with their money, and how to negotiate with the dealer that is bringing supply to the store. His parents were so happy because he turned things around for the store and things were looking better, they were seeing their profit coming in every month and were able to put more money on the loan to pay it off earlier."

Everything was working out real good for his parents and him, his parents had a chance to take a trip that they always wanted to do but could not do it because they was not making enough money from the store, and the wife work money from her job helped to keep the store stocked, the money they saved up from their son before he went to jail for the crime he did, went so fast in the business world just buying supplies and paying bills. And now that their son is home he can run the business while they are on vacation. Their son was so happy for his parent that they could have stay on vacation for a year and he would not care. All he wanted is to make showy that they enjoy their golden years before they past away.

He was very knowledgeable with the computer and set the store up on the computer system so the store can run with the days functioning of society. Some of his old friends was still coming by because they just find out that he was home, because he was not seen or heard about in any of the areas they some times go through coming from work, they was marriage and had families and moved out to the suburbs, their parents told them that he was home working at the store with his parents.

They could not believe that he was just staying in the store because he was the popular kid in the neighborhood when they were young. He told them to come back when the store close then he will be able to set and talk with them, and once the store close they set down and talk about the things that they did when they was kids and laugh, "it was his first good laugh since he was home and was glad to see the ones that was doing good things with their life."

A lot of his old friends had families and they start showing him pictures of their families that they had in their wallets, he was happy for them and they seen that he was sincere with what he was saying to them.

Then he explained; to them it's too many things out there in the street that is not real anymore and people getting caught up out there for nothing.

He said; it's not worth the time that a person will spend his whole life in prison for, just to impress other so they can think that you are trying to be something that you are not.

His friends; was very impress of what he was saying and seen how much he have grown, from a wise kid to a wise man, they all embraced each other and smile then when on their way and then he left the store and went home.

Everybody did not understand him because he was home for a year and spoke no mention of a female, the females in the communities wanted to be with him but he did not have them on his mind. He knew that most of the females was burn out from running the street and the working ones had a lot of kids and wanted to trip someone up to help them with their problems that they created on their selves.

And the ones that was all right that have good jobs that are taking care of their selves, was program by the district and federal government they work for, and he did not have time to try to reprogram a person from the thing they been doing for over ten years, he knew that it self would be a big battle that he did not want to challenge. See when he was young; he had standards that never left him, even when he was a young hustlers.

It was two kinds of female doing his time, one was a young woman that had big values with their selves, a lot of class, those was the ones he kept his self around talking to them and planning his future, because they challenge his mind and kept him thinking about what he was doing.

The other ones was the females that are controlling his city today, the fast and burn out female that have no purpose in life but to use a person for stupid things.

It seem like to him the years made the good woman's fade away, and the males was left with only one choice to be with. So he stay out of people way and if he fill the need to be with somebody he will pay for it and then go his own way with no commitments.

They knew that something was up with him because he was always a thinker and a planer and were working on something, but he would not let people know what he was thinking or planning for his self this time. His parent did not worry because they seen the positive in how he was conducting his self.

"When he was in prison all his time was studying his self and people on why do they deviate from the things that they plan for their self's, and do the opposite of what they say that would never happen to their self's. This time he plan to stay grounded and no one will be able to change him this time not even his parents, he seen a lot of things and understand why his community is in the condition that it is in, and he refuse to fall victim of society suck hole again.

He blamed the government of how the society was set up and the things they put in front of the people to trip them up, and he refuse to be tripped again being a victim of society sickness. He know that the people in his country did not understand the things that was put in front of them, they really believe that they created their problems and it were something wrong with them selves being like that. But the government will never tell them that the problem is the government and not the people, because they do not know what action to take to correct the problem that was push on the people of that country."

CHAPTER TEN

Why That I Can Not Drink And Drug Anymore

Some time when he got off from work, he rode around the community's and watched the people he use to know, the people he was watching they did not know who he were, because he was just driving through and did not stop to talk to anybody.

"The only thing he saw was a bunch of zombies that purposes were to wake up every morning; just to walk around the community's to find something to get into, just to buy something to get high off of. Their whole life was a big scheme for petty things and to try to trip some one up to slow them down, and he use to study people like them when he was in prison and still could not understand, why they could not shake that sickness off of them, and what kind of power that are holding them from waking up from the spell that is on them.

And why would these private organizations that house them in shelters, just bed them and let them return back to the street every morning, just to set around to do nothing but beg. He know that a lot of them are sick with all kinds of diseases that they been spreading around the communities where they stay, and the so call conscious people are so much in a hurry that they do not even take the time out to think about what is happening around them.

He know that a lot of shelter was being ran by some of the people that was lock up with him, the same one that thought they was rough in prison that use to stay locked up for fighting a inmate or a police officer, but now doing the same things they say that they was against, counting people, writing them up in the shelter for violations, and assigning the patience to a bed, and calling the police if one of the patience get out of hand, in doing something that the counsel feel was a violating of the company policy. They became program to be officers and they love it, all the time in prison they was just acting taught around people, just trying to do their time so no one would mess with them, they had a police mentality all the time, but was always trying to act like they was strong, he knew that something like that was gone to happen, because they was trying to be so hard in prison, trying to act like convicts, but he know that a convict will never take a officers position, all the time they was faking just trying to get by. Now the job they are doing, make them feel that they are intellectuals in thinking, just because they count people, and assign them to beds, and write the patience up for violations, and have the power to talk to the patience any kind of way.

He see that that was one part of how the weakness came in his country, with the two faced lifestyle that lead his country, having the children's to think that that is the way to be, trying to cover up their weaknesses, which one day he realize that his country will be destroy from the inside, from the two faced lifestyle that is leading the country.

He did not know how his country was in that bad of shape and could not understand why is it that the conscious could not see what's going on, they walk around the street people like they are not there and use them for their own selfish purpose.

He was trying to figure out the things that they was using them to do, and if they did the math they would see it's not worth the time, because letting a person stay in those condition just for some one to benefit off of, they will see more people giving up on their self and the country would start decaying all around them."

"And the other country's that's against his country will see *the opportunity to take the vantage of a good thing for them, and a bad thing for his country. He still could not figure out why do people need to have so mush power over other just for them to feel good, and do power make you lose focus on the things that is happening right in front of your face?*

Is his country going throw a mental problem that they do not know what to do, or is the past mistake that was made, leaving his country in a way that they can not shake it off, to make a better future."

"He watched some people and seen that they was so scare *of where they might be at next, in the street with out a job or living in situation where they living just for paying bill and nothing else.*

Everybody is walking light because they know at anytime that it can happen to them and they can be walking the street just for a little of nothing.

Everybody trying to find some kind of hobby to keep their minds off of what they know, because no one could help them to understand what is going on, and their kids have got so backward trying to relive the past of what their parents did when they was young, and the parents are encouraging them to act like that.

He seen that their parents are not ashamed of their ways because that is all they know, and they always want their child to look up to them, even if it might be the cause of their child life, it seems like to him that the parents are dependent on their kids for everything, good things and bad things, the good so call things they are looking for the kids to get a good job when they get out of college to buy them a house and take care of them for the rest of their life, and the bad things are that the parents let the kids hustle out in front of their house because the kid help them out with some of their bills and other needs that they have."

The ones that went to prison with him he seen some of them, but they did not see him, they lose so mush weight that he almost could not recognize them, he even saw one of them when he was at a red light, they ran up to a car and started washing the front window, he just looked at him and drove of when the light turn greed.

Later he found out that some of them was living in shelters and all they do is drink and drug, the young hustlers been slapping them around treating them like they was a mop rag.

He could not understand what was going on because his crew did a lot of good things in the communities to bring the *young kids in to consciousness, then to turn around and see that the young hustlers can not take the time out to think about what they are doing to the ones that would help them more then hurt them, he realize that the people in his country have taking a negative position to self destroy their own country.*

He knew that the weak and stupid hustlers had something to do with that and turning the street back to the police officers and people that came from other places, people coming from other places was more respected then the ones that fought to keep the people out from other places, coming in their communities trying to take over. Like that old saying (there's no honor amongst thieves) the young hustlers was so out of control because their leader was some scare fouls that had control over all the young hustlers in the city.

"They were robbing each other and killing one another taking each other females and the old hot hustlers that were controlling the weak and stupid hustlers enjoyed every bit of it. See they were so busy in destroying each other, they did not have time to "think and see and try to figure out who was creating the problem that they was going through."

He knew that was one thing in his life that will never happen again, was to go back in the street hustling, he felt that it will take the rest of a "person life to try to correct the way they mess up the streets to day, and he did not want that responsibility, because he knew that project would be a death sentence for some one who take it on."

He knew that person will be locked up for the rest of his life, "because they had to kill a lot of people to get order back in the city," where people can be safe to walk the streets again, they had older people to scare to set on their porches and little kids could not play out side.

But he know that something had to happen to make a change and it was not gone to come from the "government," it had to happen from the "communities" the ones that is concern about the things that is happening in their neighborhoods.

Now he see the opportunity to make his move on the city, but still it was going to take some time for him to set everything in motion, first he have to find the concern people that will act and not talk, and then form a group to protect the community from the out side forces and go to the government and ask for a loan to build their community back up with the people that they can hirer and firer.

Then he have to go to each house door to door and talk with the old neighbors in the neighborhood, of the thing that they are trying to do and in the future when things get better they will be calling on them, for some assistance to improve the community more better for the future of the kids that will be coming behind them.

By the city being so mess up he did not know where to start, the first thought came to his mind was at the store, because the people that come in to buy products are health conscious, so he start talking to some of the customers just to see where their minds were at, some had good thoughts and some had thoughts that the creator put them on earth just to live their time out in peace and harmony.

One day a person that shop in the store came in to shop and talked with him and asked if he could come to a meeting with him to night when he get off from work.

He accepted the invitation; and when the store close he met with the person, when they got to the meeting he walked in and seen a lot of people setting in chairs lessoning to a person that was talking about the thing that he was thinking about.

He set down and lesson the whole time he was there and did not say a thing to the person that brought him there, then after it was over the person that brought him there introduced him to some of the people that was there and the person who were talking came up and introduce his self to him.

He started feeling real good like he was some where that he always wanted to be at but never could find it.

After the meeting he went home and every time they had a meeting he was there and he got to know everybody that was there, the ones he thought was more aggressive he was moving more towards them to spend a lot of his time around them talking about things in the communities.

Most of them was self employ and always got together a lot of time with the kids of the communities to do all kinds of activities and teach the kids how to do thing to survive that school did not teach.

He was invited from some of the members in the meeting to go with them and the kids to places and talk to some of the kids, he was watching the kids to see who was the leader of them so he could spend a lot of time with them, he know if the leaders of the kids was taught to be positive the rest will follow them and will do everything they do just to get their approval.

He ended up spending a lot of time with some of the kids, and ended up having some of them work in the store with him when they was out of school, he was real strict with them and allow them to do their home work from school in the store before they started working, and told them that their time start when they finest their home work and he had to check it to make show that it was right. They knew that the work had to be right or they will be there all day doing it and would not be able to work.

One day he was at the meeting and the person that be speaking all the time called him up to speak to the crowd, it was a surprise to him but he was waiting for this day to come so he can speak.

He went up on the stage and thanked the speaker for giving him a chance to talk about the things that are on his mind.

He knew that his words had to be real soft and not speak about what he really feel, so he talked about the kids that he hire to work in his family store and the progress they are making, to be better people in the future.

Then he said; I remember a saying on some one shirt that was shopping at my family store, it was saying "each one teach one" that it self made me think about how many people that's walking around in the communities, that feel like we do but do not know what to do, if it wouldn't for one of the member here taking the time to watch my energy and talk to me I would not be here. He give me my life back and opened up doors that I always dream about of wanting to do these things that you all are doing. But I did not know where to start at or who to see, I had the opportunity to see the kids and play with them and try to teach them the ways for our future to exist.

I will be thanking that member for the rest of my life because I want him to know that I appreciate him for taking the time out of his life and putting me in it, and that I will do everything in my power so he will know that the time he took out of his life was not wasted on me.

Then he thank the speaker for being knowledgeable on all the things that is going on in our communities and then gave the speaking back to the speaker and went back to be seated.

He set back and watch the people out of the side of his eyes to see if they was watching him, and the speaker said lets thank the brother for giving that good speech, and that I would like him to come and speak all the time, everybody started clapping and was saying yes we would like to hear more of his speaking to.

He know that his plan was working and he had a place with them in the future he will try to make them trust him a hundred percent, and they will know that he is real loyal to the communities in the city, and want to find away to build it back up for the people.

The next time he spoke at the meeting, his words was more into the things that he would like to say, but was still soft words so they could understand the things without them thinking that he was to aggressive.

He said; I like to talk on "transformation and evolving" see we was created by a thought like the seed that we plant in the ground, than that thought had to be feed to nourish and to protect it from the things that can break down the seed, and weaken it from developing the way it suppose to be, those seeds are like animals that have baby's when they bring them into the world to watch over them.

The animals go to a place where all the animals go that are peaceful with each other to drink water and eat, they are in harmony with each other and they move around freely not feeling threaten by one another. But the animal are like that seed we planted in the ground some time the weeds get in and try to take over the seeds that started growing and rap them selves around the seeds that's growing and destroy them. Some of the bad animals go where they know the peaceful animals go at to find food, but the peaceful animals can sense that someone is around them that do not mean them any good, that when they all try to stick together to protect each other from getting eaten.

But you will always see that the bad animals all the time will go after the weakest link in the crowd that can not keep up. And the time pasted so fast that he could not finish with what he was saying so they whole it off to the next meeting, but everybody clapped and was so excited for the next meeting to come.

When the next meeting came the speaker give him the floor for the whole day, he knew then that he made progress with the group at the meeting. He open up saying that let me take the time out to think you for letting me share my thoughts with the group, and started back on the animals and the seeds and said we are like them both, we try to protect our seeds and try to nourish our children's that come from our seeds.

But today society refuse to help us take good care of both the seed and the child by putting cigarettes and alcohol into our communities stores and programming us from a kid that that is all right to do these things once a person get older.

But our government they know the problem that it will bring in the communities and start destroying our bodies little by little, but our biggest problem would be our kids that grow up with so much hate for their parents they are the ones who will be the victims first and will be able to influence the other kids.

Before you know it they be talking back at the parents and trying to fight them, and then parent will not no what to do but let that kid act out to they see it the hard way. By that time the kid will be grow and the communities are messed up with all kinds of problems that kid grow up with thinking everything was all right that they did.

Then he close the meeting out by saying I have a big family now and glad to be a part of my new siblings and we have to take care of our new nephew and niece, than they left from the meeting.

The next day some of the kids that work in the store parents came in to think him for letting their sons and daughters work, and giving them responsibilities, because they seen a great improve in their kids. He asks them could they come to a meeting with him because he wanted them to hear the things that were being talked about and they accepted to go with him.

CHAPTER ELEVEN

Why That I Can Not Give My Responsibilities To Someone Else

The day of the meeting he went over the kids house to pick their parents up and to drive them to the meeting, the parents was a little nervous because they did not know what to expect. When they arrive one of the members came and gives him a hug than the other members came one by one hugging him, he was a little worried because he did not see the speaker of the group, and asked where the speaker at, and what is going on?

And one of the member said to him the speaker moved on to another city, and than gave him all the keys that the speaker had of everything door or lock that the speaker had to open up.

Than the member said; he left all the responsibility to you to be the speaker of our group for now on. He was so overwhelm with excitement that he had to set down for a minute to catch his breath because now he know that they really trust him. The people that he brought with him they was quiet, because they could not understand what was going on, then one of the members said it was time for the speaker to leave, but he had to stay to he find somebody that could take over his position for him.

He looked at some of the people that was there way before he came on board, and they all said to him we was not ready to take that responsibility, than one said it was so many things that he would had to teach us with so little of time you was a god send, because he were call on to leave us about a year ago, but he stay because he did not want us to drift backward and let things get out of hand.

Then one said; I am proud to admit that I am not ready to be a represented over people life's, I have a little more to learn in the patient department, and the other said the same thing with a smile and was not a shame to admit it.

One member said; I know that you wanted to see the speaker before he left, but this is how he function, he will pop in and out of your life at any time and set down and talk with you like he never left your sight, he not a man that believe in fare wells with people that he attached his self to.

Than the meeting started; and he said life is full of surprises and you have to be ready for them when they come, to day I just was bringing my family in to meet with the family and my brothers and sisters surprise me with this, I will do everything in my power not to let my family down.

One thing about the speaker who left, knew he was a man who can use his words well, and in the future he will be able to build a big congregation that will spread through the city.

Then he said; my brothers and sisters that I brought here today are the mother and father of our nephews and nieces that we work with in preparing them to take over our cities one day.

I want my brothers and sisters to know that we are with them in lending a helping hand to help shape the future in our young, because we know that our government will take all of their time in working for them and leave our kids to grow up by their self's.

That's why we have to be responsible in governing our self's in to what direction our future will go in our communities around us. We have to learn how to keep the money in the neighborhood, see our money leaves the community on the first cycle when we spend it, as long as we continual in letting that happen our communities will never grow, that's like putting a baby tree and burying it in the ground with clay for soil, there will be no nourishments for the tree to sustain, because the clay will stop the nourishment from getting to the roots of that tree.

That is what our government are doing to the country and we been program to fight each other as long as it became a part of our life that we understand, and than when we realize that something are wrong we will be to old to do anything about it.

Than he said; when I was incarcerated yes imprison for being a young hot headed kid like some we see today. Some of the members knew that but other did not know it but did not care because they feel good about him, and the parents that came with him did not worry about it either because they had experience with people that was imprisoned and came out to do good things for the community.

Than he continue by saying; a older man was there with me that I always talked to, that older person told me the government do not really like people with values and principles, they only keep them around to watch their business and money but treat those people real bad.

Then the older person said to me have you ever thought why people come home from work and drink their self to sleep, than wake up in the morning and go the work and do the process all over again, those loyal people can not understand why is their boss are treating them like that, when they know that the work around the company are getting done by the one they treat bad.

Than the older person said; our government is the biggest trader in the country, he said look at the entertainment world they have every actor acting a act that in their real life they are the opposite of the act, they betraying to the communities making the young kids get so confuse in how they suppose to be.

The older person said; that why we see so many people drinking and drugging because the country is confusing them and taking the advantage over their kids and they know it but can not do nothing about it. It's almost like slavery we bring our children in the world just for the master to do what they want to them. So people have to medicate their self every day because they do not want to see it, and know if they try to say something about it they will be without a job, so they suck it up and role with the way the country is going being programmed to look the other way.

See that's how the government trick our young, because we as adults feel the recession but our kids do not really feel it or understand it, because we are their protectors so they would not feel it, and when they finish school and take a job to start their life as adults, they still will not feel it because our recession will be their adjustment.

They will adjust to the bad conditions as a normal way the country is and will be able to function with out any problem.

Why because your bill is eighty percent higher then theirs, they are like a new burn baby just learning how to walk. Ten years from now than they will start feeling the recession for them self's, than the cycle will be repeated over and over again, the country will always be in a recession but the generation behind you would never know it at that time.

That's how our government trick us to make us think that progress have been made and the country is working it's self out of the recession.

But when you start thinking that the crisis is over all you have to do is go down to the department of finance office and find out what the dollar is worth in all the countries that we owe debt to.

We have to build a financial network right here in our community's, where we can go at and get loans from the community, it will be a co-op corporation that we can loan our own money to each other for starting your own business up, or when a person need a loan to consolidate all the loan they have from other lender with high interest rates.

Our interest rates will be the lowest in the country, because we will not be profiting off of each other, we will assign a committee to over see the business with about twenty members working to watch where our money go.

We will have to vote in the ones that the group want to manage our business, you always have to take into consideration that the members that we pick might decline from being a manager for other reason that have nothing to do with their loyalty for the group, like some members did to day with me being elected to be the speaker of the group.

I myself recognizes their loyalty; he than said, they were just tested and did not know it, a hypocrite would have took that position for all the wrong reason, like they say if you really want to find strength in a person you have to test them when they do not know it, you can put that person in bad conditions with all kinds of temptations around them to weaken them and they still come out smelling like a rose.

Than he close by saying; that we have to start treating our communities like we treat our new born child with a lot of love and protection, doing that than we will be able to program our kids from day one to act responsible in everything they do and they will never disrespect their *community for no out side force, that will try to use their money to divide us like a chess piece and having us fight each other so they can sneak in and steal our power from us.*

The next day at his store people start coming from every where to shop there, shacking his hand and saying I will be at the next meeting. He finely opens the door up for the opportunity of communicating with the communities and gains their trust for the thing he would like to do in the communities. And his parents was so shock how their inventory grown over night and the amount they was making a day, they was so excited for the things that was occurring for the store and most of all for the son they have, that left them as a boy and came back a man.

They hire more kids to work in the store and the kids were so happy to interact with the public in finding products for them. He organize the computer system so good that he put each young kid in the computer with a different code, they had to lodge in everyday for the work they done, that will stop him asking what each one did and they would not be able to get credit for something they did not do.

He and his parents let the kids run the cash register and did not worry about nothing, because the son program the cash register for everybody that get on it to lodge in on their code, so if there was a mistake that happen they can go right to it and the person who made it.

His parents told him that they was proud of what he were doing with the kids, and he said to them the things you both installed in me I hope it will make you happy in seeing your work, and if I can be a example to show the parents of to day that if they stay on course with their kids nothing but good thing can follow it.

CHAPTER TWELVE

Why That I Can Not Be A Lover

At the next meeting his parents came to surprise him, they was setting in the back so he could not see them, the meeting was starting to get real crowded with so many people that came from every where, the crowd was out the door and on to the side walk, they had to walk around the neighborhood to get permission from the community to put speakers in the window.

By the weather being good the members brought folded chairs out and borrowed some from the church that was down the street, to accommodate the people that could not get in to hear the speaker speak, his parents could not believe what they were seeing and his mother started crying by witnessing the trust the people have for her son.

He spoke and said; the day is a good one for us all that came and lets look around each other and see who your brothers and sisters of all races that came to answer the call for unity, to bring our communities in harmony with the universe.

Just saying; that little bite cars was stopping at first they were slowing down to see what was going on, when he started talking everything came to a stop some of the member in the meeting had to go out and direct the traffic for the other cars could go through.

This was a day that surprised everybody they was not ready for what was happening, but the speaker took action quick and fast like a captain on a ship he position his group and divided them in to four sections.

Two section; worked in side ones section was putting the chairs close, why the other ones was showing them where to be seated at.

The two out side sections; one was bringing chairs out to put on the grass and sidewalk, while the other ones was taking care of the traffic.

Then he spoke; let me say to our government that this is a day where all the tribes of the city came out together in harmony and peace to find a solution to our problem in this city.

He spoke and said; that we the people are fed up with you telling us lies and frost hope that our kids can not live off of, our constitution of this country allow us to find a solution to our problem in a "peaceful" way, when the government brake down and can not fix their self to start back up in a "constructive" way. Pushing all kinds of free food in the communities is doing nothing but making us depended on businesses who companies are in this country that are from other countries who are profiting good here.

I can not understand where are all this food is coming in from feeding the country but you say there are no jobs for the people of this country, let's tell the people the truth that we are a "discontinue" model watch is not needed anymore, and that you the government do not know what to do with "as the government will put it the waste anymore."

But I have to say our government problem came from us, why I say us because when it's time to elect a official to run for office we always pick only the two parties that we was program to see.

And they will "cut your wound wide open" and tell you that they putting something in it to make things better for you "than poured salt in it," and we was so programmed to believe everything they say, we start to think that the salt is helping us. And to top it off we will start trying to convince other around us that things are better now since the remedy they use to enter in our bodies, "but it was salt and nothing else" and the new ailments that is happening to our bodies we think it's coming from something else than the salt.

Because we was program to believe that our government officials will never do us any harm, but I am here to tell you that's a lie and we see it every day, but ignore the things around us like we do our children. We can find everything wrong with our neighbor kids, but our child might be the leader of them all and still could not see it, it's easy for us to blame some one else for our problems that we created ourselves. We open the corporate door in to our communities with no restrictions for them to follow, but to do what they want to our communities, then we ask ourselves what's gone on in our communities and how did this get so fare out of control with out us seeing it.

Like I witness in some neighborhood all these males with the "fly out fits" on, that be getting money from those female who work, and some might take it from females that get government assistance, taking from the child mouth and do not care "better yet they laugh about it" calling the female stupid, because when every month comes he there with his hand out with another scheme of how he gone to turn the money in to two or three times of what they got from them.

Or you might run across a male that have kids from five different females that he think is cool to do, because there something wrong with him, and all he do to those females are lie to them, but we can not blame him for the things he do, because they was program to be like that, and that those female play a part when they know that he have all those kids from different females, some might say they did not know but it's hard for me to believe that, because if he brought them around his family some of the members was trying to tell her but she was not listing.

Then we have the females think she can sleep around with every male they can get with, had babies by at lease five different males, but when she get burned out they find a victim that remember her from yesteryears and he fall in the trap, the bad part about the victim he just walk in and acquired the sins that the Creator had for her, in over words all of her pain will go to him, because he is the protector of all of her sins she committed on her self.

Then the speaker said; I can go on and on but we catch on fast and get the picture, see what I am saying everybody got use to the same lies because we dying for some hope, but we looking in the wrong place for hope my brothers and sisters.

If you have an abused parent all your life you not gone to bring your children around them, for they to watch your kids while you at work. But to day it seem like that is happening in one out of ten house hole today, and they adjusted to it because that is the normal thing everybody is doing ignoring the problem, because to them it's not a problem anymore it became a adjustment and people got adjusted to the sickness and now it's normal.

See program is like a disease that we can not control I do not care how much you thing that you got everything under control,

I hate to say it my brother and sister you do not, see we been condition from a child by our parents and our communities and the TV, so everything that come out of your mouth have already been prepared for us to fall in one of those categories, they design for us to be that way so they can control and supervise all your time with you not knowing it.

He said; believe me my brother and sister when I say fall in, like some of the worker that work for the government or private businesses they will stab each other in the back so fast for a position, some might have been raised up with each other from a kid, but will not care if that person is in their way trying to get to the top.

And the bad part about it they will laugh with the others that are around them, who play apart destroying that person and convincing their self's it was the right thing to do, and the ones that come out from prisons they been watched by the government for years they know which ones are weak and strong, because when they was in prison the officers and counsels use to right down notes on every inmate on what they did, and what they heard about them doing, and kept that information as a ace in the hole for when they return back to society the government know how to position their self's in dealing with that person.

See those people are program not to understand the truth and if they was told it, they will swear you down that everything we are talking about is a lie, because they are programmed not to face the truth and every time they hear something like the truth they run, see those people are so scare of the truth because they running from a secrete, that they do not want other to know about in their past, but the government know and putted them in position to run the business for them because they have control over them.

See it do not take a rocket science to know that a person who will do something to the people that have their back is a weak person and can be control by anybody with power. And that is who the government is programming to position them to be in front of the conscious ones in the communities to control our way of thinking.

Then he said; doing closing it's time for us all to know our weaknesses and the weaknesses of the company we keep around us as friends. Because they are the ones we will bring around our families to meet and if they have any kind of sickness it's a good chance that it will spread to your families. And by the time you find out about it your kids might be grown and starting their life out with children's, repeating the things they learn from your friend that you brought around your families. It's a disease that got to be caught and controlled before it get out and destroy the communities we live in.

We as family members of the communities will have to do the same things that the officer did to the prisoner in prison, write down what is happening in your neighborhood and watch who spending a lot of time with the kids when there's no other adults around them.

Find out who that person is and what do they do for a living, and stop putting your time on a person that mind their business, they can not do any harm to you because they are mining their own business and not yours, so what did the government tell you to watch about that person, something that he or she might tell you about what your government is doing to you, we have been programmed to watch the wrong things, and the things we should be watching happening in front of us every day.

Then he stop; and everybody came up to shake his hand and left the meeting and the people from the out side came in to see him to shake his hand, he looked up and realize his parents were there and he smile and they smile and left. One thing the adults did not know that when he is at the store with the kids, they be having a different meeting then the adults have, he be giving them information of things to prepare them different then he is preparing the adults. He knew the strength are in the young and not the old and they one day will have to take over the new technology world that the old would not have patience for.

One day in the store a preacher came in and ask could he talk with him?

"And he said yes."

Than preach; told him they are having a meeting later on and would like for him to attain?

"He accepted the invitation;" and when the store closed he when down to the church on the street where they hole their meeting at. When he walked in they were setting around like they are waiting on him. That's when he realizes the

meeting is about him. He went in and introduced his self and they introduced their self's and one of the preachers said lets get down to business he got quiet and listen to what they had to say.

Then one of the preachers asks; him how much money was he making at his meeting?

He was surprised in how they were talking to him but was not surprised of what they was saying, but he stay silence and allow them to keep burying their self's.

Then one said; we can help you get a lot of money if you work with us?

"He spoke; and asks what would that be?"

Then one preacher said; I heard that you are getting everybody together and going to open up a community co op lending company to set money in for the purpose to serve the community needs?

"And he said; yes we are looking in to something like that."

"The preacher said; it would be beneficial for him if he put them on the board to watch over the money."

"He asked; why do you think that?"

"The preacher said; because we have the government officials in our back pocket, and they what you to know

through us they will work on pasting anything you bring to them."

He heard enough and said; we are working with the communities it have nothing to do with the government so how did we get there.

Then one preacher said; I see that you are hard to convince, but name your price and we can try to accommodate it for you, because everybody has a price that they are looking for?

"He said; my price is helping the communities bring better education back in the schools, keeping the money in the communities, and letting our money develop the communities for our kids in the future, and stop making the communities be dependent on hand out from other countries, and closed it up by saying can you accommodate that?"

They all got quiet and did not say anything then he looks around at each and every one of them, and said I guest not, and then he walked out of the church.

He knew that was his first challenge with the government and that more will be coming his way. He prepare his self for this day and knew the things that was going to come with the actions he taking, and prepared his parents for it, and told them that there will be a lot of opposition against the truth so be prepare for anything that might come his way.

CHAPTER THIRTEEN

Why That I Can Not Be Gay

That day of the next meeting he walked in and the members seen something was worrying him, the place was pack again and people was out side waiting to get in, or for them to bring chairs out for them. He told the members to try to accommodate them without borrowing any chairs from the church then he went up to speak, the members knew that something was on his mind because he was not in a good move at all.

Then he said; good day my brothers and sisters it's a pleasure to be amongst the ones that love nursing our plants in the communities.

To day I like to talk on "opposition" that is a word that we take for granted, but we should not be sleeping on that word. Because the force that is behind it is powerful and will trick you if you are not conscious of your surroundings, that opposition force will wait for the right time to make their move on you when they think it's the right time. I had a meeting with some high officials of the communities and they ask me to let them be apart of the co op that we are working on, I allow them to talk, and I listen in what they had to say about the co op and how they feel about the communities. Then one of them said; to me it will be beneficial for me if I can put them on the board to manage the company.

Then I ask them; to tell me the benefits for the communities and not for me and the room turn silence then I left the meeting and rode around the neighborhood for a while then went home for the day.

Then he said; do you know what make the "opposition" so powerful today is because we not fighting back, they know that the people are so vulnerable in the communities that they set traps up for you to walk in them. That day of the meeting with some high officials they set the trap up for me, but I seen it because when I walked in they were setting around waiting for me, so the whole meeting was just about me and not the communities because they would have started the meeting without me.

Then he said; what is wrong with these high officials in this city all they see is how much money they can make out of the deal.

Then he said; the next word we take for granted is "unconscious," we walk a around our communities not conscious of what is taking place every day, we allow disease into our lives to break our bodies down and mess with our heads by not being conscious of the situation that is in front of us everyday. See what the government do is create situations for the communities for us to fall in them, then they pass it to the "opposition" to set them up to trap us in the web they created, but in order to make it work right they have to get our minds off of being conscious to trap our communities.

So they put all kinds of "unconscious" obstacles in our way so we can get use to them and then they become apart of our everyday life. Then we will play our own part in destroying our community's life, we will be thinking that we are functioning normal in the way we see the country suppose to be going.

See when they integrated this country from segregation the government broke up the unity that some communities had with each other, did the government know that would happen, I can not say they did or did not. But I can say that they did predict our future of which way they want the country to go, and how things should be in the order they see fit.

Having that much power over the country they have so call "genius" predicting the future, having inventors inventing technology for the future to make a better place for tomorrow, but these well educated peoples can not find a way to make the world better then what it is today.

Instead of the government making better schools in every community, they integrated people that were not ready for that change so fast.

By being segregated so long they thought that it was the way of life for them, just from that move it self chaos was created and everything that was, became a thing of the past, racial disorder started and the country took a spin in the way our government thought was right for the people.

But they was experimenting with our lives and here are today rescores that came from that experiment, a lot of hate is still here and segregation, a lot of trickery still here and broking schools where kids are not getting good educations, forcing different lifestyles down people throats, pushing disease on the communities by making decisions for the country that is bad, and forcing them to take prescription drugs that is damaging their organs.

Our government became a trader to the natural things and forced us to be apart of betraying the natural things, and made us recognizes the artificial world first to live by and stand for.

Then to top it off they put the artificial lifestyle in front of the natural lifestyle to control our every move, and if you get out of line the artificial lifestyle have the power to destroy you and the law will call it a criminal act that one done against the country just for being natural.

So the people got condition to working with the artificial lifestyle so long that it became apart of their everyday life, now when they see someone that is doing natural things they think that something is wrong with them.

But something suppose to be wrong with them because our government said that the artificial lifestyle have a choice to do anything they want to do, but the government made all natural things something that people look at as being against the laws or strange for acting natural in his country.

See pushing the people into integrate made us more segregated then ever, you might walk in a store where the workers do not want to wait on you, see I am different then you I leave because I do not want to be some ware where they dislike me for no reason, and I know that I am not gone to eat their food they made food me. Forcing people to make decision was not a choice of their own and a lot of hate came behind it, the worse kind of hate came with it the ones that you can not see when it hit.

I believe that "segregation" is a bad thing because you will be "depriving" others of the opportunity that the country have for them, and "integration" was a forced thing trying to put others together to function on the same level that they was not ready for, and "separation" should be a choice thing, others should have a right to function with people who they are comfortable with.

But our government again does things for the wrong reason it's all about the biggest groups in the country, bigger the groups are more votes you will have when you go their way. See our country is so backward and confuse in the things they be doing, you can buy alcohol that's all right, a female can get a baby sucked out of her stomach that's all right, you can see a male make love to another male and a female make love to another female but that's all right.

But if you see a person grow natural drugs in their back yard or house it's against the law, if you see a person try to function normal and stay to their self you is wrong for thinking like that, if a person try to group up with people that will try to better their communities without the government say, you wrong, if you try to correct your kid in a way that the government do not approve of, then you wrong.

The person that is trying to kill his or her self have more rights then a person who want to live the normal life.

He said; see the problem to day we are looking for a leader that can take care of our problem, but that will not help us anymore, our leaders came and went the Prophets and Messengers but we are still in the same mess, what we really need for our communities are strength and organizational skills, so when we do something it will stay in the communities, and we will not lose it when we elect some one in office and they decide to change things.

Then he close saying; look around you and see who right there because that day is coming when we will have to need one another, you might see someone that is close to your neighborhood or on the street with you it's time to get together and work on building your area around you.

Then he said; as of the day all of our bad habits that is slowing us up, it's time to start working on them, because if we love each other then it's not hard to let go our enemies that we helping to destroy our communities.

Then everybody left the meeting and he close the building up and was walking to his car, a "police officer" drove up and looked at him with a real hard hate look and said to him you talk to much then drove off fast, he knew that was a "intimidation" move to go with the program or else. Then he drove home for the night to retire so he can get up to open the store in the morning.

CHAPTER FOURTEEN

Why That I Can Not Follow The Crowd

When he got to the store that morning everything that happened to him leaving from the meeting yesterday was still on his mind, he call all the kids together and talk to them and told his parents what took place yesterday when he went home that night from the meeting.

He said; to the kids things we was talking about are close and everything might change real fast, see we do not have control over how some people view us or what they say about us. See it's a lot of misguided peoples out there that is waiting for the opportunity to destroy you at anytime when they get a chance, but you have to be alert to watch out for all things because you will never know which way they are coming, and if you see it you still might can not stop it, so do not never for get your teaching we always talked about, it's that time to start practicing them as of today.

Then he said; do not for get about strength, and structure, and organizational skills, that one needs to keep with them at all time, it will open your eyes and guide you to better things in the future, study the people that come in your surrounding to try and find exactly why they really are around you.

Then he left; them in the back doing the work that they suppose to be doing. He went up to the front to open the door for the customers to come in and start shopping in the store. One of the customer came in and stop to talk with him like he do all the time for the last two months, before he start shopping for the things he need. He talked to him about a project that he was getting off the ground and wanted to know what did he think about it, and that he would like for him to look at it when he get a chance.

The customer said; I have it out in the car and I can bring it in and leave it with you for a day or two, and when you have time you can check it out and tell me what you think about it?

"He said ok to the customer and the customer ran out to the car to get it."

"Three minutes after the customer left a person came in and walked up to the counter and pull out a gun and shot him two times in the head and two times in the chess," "then

ran out to a car that was Double Parked waiting for him and took off down the back streets in the neighborhood." Everybody ran from the back to see what just happen and the customers was running out the store seaming and crying "helloing" help some one call the police, some one just shot the owner of the store. The kids and his parents surrounded him and waited for the ambulance to come and get him, because they knew he was gone, they were so organizes when they came out it looked like a fire drill test that they give you in school, two of the kids went out front of the door to protect the front and see if they can see the shooter, business owner that was on the block with them came up to the front of the store to see and ask what happen.

The two young kids did not say anything about what happened in side they ask did anybody see somebody leaving out after they heard the shots. A lot of business owners describe what the heard and seen and some people were walking on the street told what they seen after the shots. The police officers came fast and surrounded the area and got information from the people that was out in the street when the incident happen, the police officers got a description of what kind of car they was driving and put out alert to the other officers to be on a look out for the car, his parents was real calm *and alert to what was taking place and knew that the police officers was not there for their son best interests.*

It was so many police officers and about three helicopter in the sky searching for the car that the shooter got away in, but the parents and the kids knew that was just a front for the community, they knew that the shooter was not going to be caught because they feel that the police officers had something to do with it.

The ambulance came to pick him up he was dead when the parents and the kids came out from the back. After the police officers did their report on the incident the parents and the kids closed the door and locked it, then they went in the back and hugged one another and then started crying, they feel it was time to let it out around the people that they are comfortable with.

At the funeral peoples came from every where it was so crowded that the police officers was there to control the traffic that was pouring in.

The speaker who use to speak at the meetings where he was speaking at that elected him to be the speaker for the meeting came and spoke in his behalf, he was the first one to speak who open it with saying today is a "day of life not death," the good brother energy brought all good energies together to day like he always did when he would be speaking at the meeting.

I elected the good brother because the first day I saw him at the meeting it was something about him I felt, and every time he came back to the meeting, I felt stronger and stronger about him, then one day I wanted to see what did he know so I called him up to speak and his energy had a force so powerful it let me know, here is the speaker that I was looking for to replace me. Everything that I wanted to do, or was trying to do, but did not have enough time to do it. I finally found someone that can take my place, who I can leave my brothers and sisters with, and know that they will be protected.

Who ever done this, think that they did something to stop the movement, then my misguided brother you showily have been mislaid, but if you any where around us I want them to know by looking at the powerful force of unity that he brought together that no negative force can take from us. See they thought that by killing the good brother the message would be lost, but if they would have came to the meetings when he was speaking, they would have heard in some of his speeches, that we are not looking for a Messenger anymore because our Messengers and Prophets have already came, we are looking for strength and organizational skills, to bring about harmony in our communities, and that is something you can not kill only the communities can do that to their self's, by letting the truth die with the good brother.

But that will be impossible because the truth find it's way back home like water find a crack to come through, you can not close the truth out of life, because the truth is life and if it do not exist anymore then life will end.

See that's one thing negative force do not understand, and we will waste our time trying to explain it to them, because they do not have the things in them which is called "reason", "the reason to do things better," "the reason a good brother was born into life," "the reason the rain come to earth," "the reason," that is a word that the negative force will never understand because they was not program to have a "reason" for trying to do something positive. If they were then it would have been easy for them to see that they can not stop the "reason" by killing someone.

Then the old speaker stop talking and he looked at the "police officers" that was inside, then a lot of the members were looking at them, the police officers were so uncomfortable, they left out and stay on the out side of the building.

Then the speaker said; that he was speaking for his parents and the young brothers and sisters who allow him to take up all of the time and I am sorry if someone else wanted to speak, but I got be side my self because I am up set about this, but it's time to take our brother home so lets care our brother through the communities for everybody to know, and the traffic will stop and line up with us to bring him to his resting place where he will be retire at.

Then everybody left out to go to their cars and when they open the door to leave it was cars lined up blocking the street for about five long blocks, and peoples was lined up on the sidewalk of both sides from block to block, his parents had no ideal that their son touched this many peoples in his life.

CLOSING STATEMENT

A lot of people were coming to the store to meet with his parents to think them for raising a knowledgeable son, and some came to share stories with them of the things that their son did for them when he was off from work, and rode around the community before he went home. It was a side of him that he was doing for the communities that a lot of his members did not know.

He would drive around when he get off from work and spot a problem kid and set down and talk with that kid for hours, then the kid will introduce him to his parents or parent, then he will make it his business to try and get the parents feel free to speak their problems with him. Some parents he will get into a heavy argument with, but before he leave them he will say things to them like you can argue with me everyday, but I am coming back because you my brothers and sisters and I will fight to the end so you can see what the system is doing to your family.

The members that was with his group they had a lot of visitors from the church, preachers trying to convince them that what happen to him came from his past when he was a young hustler, and that they talk with him a lot of times about the co op lending program that they was trying to put together, and he was gone to make the church preachers the head of the board.

Then a preacher said; I did not really trust him because he never talked about how he can help the peoples in the communities. The members never did anything with the preachers of the churches but refuse to talk with them when they call.

The young kids at the store ended up opening five more store around the communities for his parents, and started their own organization with the young kids. Some of the young kids groups were too radical so they broke off from the other and left the store because they did not want to bring trouble to them.

The others was semi radical and stay to communicate with the other kids around the communities, and you had some was strictly business they turned the stores to a top of the line heath food stores and turn the business to a franchise. All the kids that was working at the store they had one thing in common the dislike for the "law and the people have to take control of their life in order to make a difference in their communities.

The communities drifted back to there bad habits in time because the force was more powerful then them, one person could not change a city when they was program to quiet before they reach their goals, and they never got the co op off the ground the preachers play apart in that not happening, they never could get the government officials in the city to approve it to come in the city for the communities.

The adults started losing consciousness but the young kids started getting stronger, the things he told the kids they did it and did not let the adult know anything that they was doing, because they seen the things that he said what would happen with the adults and it came to be true.

Thanks for taking the time out to read this fictional story, I did not name any corridors because it can be anybody you know, and I did not name a country because it can be any country , and I did not name a race because it can be any race you in.